KU-599-232

This book belongs to:

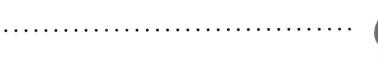

....

....

Retold by Sue Graves
Illustrated by Gwyneth Williamson

Reading consultants: Betty Root and Monica Hughes

Marks and Spencer p.l.c.
PO Box 3339
Chester, CH99 9QS

shop online
www.marksandspencer.com

ISBN 978-1-84805-317-5
Printed in China

First Readers

Snow White and the Seven Dwarfs

MARKS &
SPENCER

Helping your child to read

First Readers are closely linked to the National Curriculum. Their vocabulary has been carefully selected from the word lists recommended by the National Literacy Strategy.

Read the story

Read the story to your child a few times.

Long ago, there was a girl called Snow White.
Snow White was pretty.
She lived with her father, the king, and her stepmother, the queen.
The queen was pretty.
But not as pretty as Snow White.

8

Follow your finger

Run your finger under the text as you read. Your child will soon begin to follow the words with you.

Look at the pictures
Talk about the pictures. They will
help your child to understand the story.

Snow White was pretty.

9

Have a go
Let your child
have a go at
reading the large
type on each
right-hand page.
It repeats a line
from the story.

Join in
When your child is ready,
encourage them to join in with the
main story text. Shared reading is
the first step to reading alone.

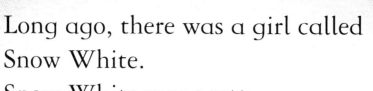

Long ago, there was a girl called
Snow White.
Snow White was pretty.
She lived with her father, the king, and
her stepmother, the queen.
The queen was pretty.
But not as pretty as Snow White.

Snow White was pretty.

The queen had a magic mirror.
She looked in her magic mirror.
"Who is the fairest?" said the queen.
"Snow White," said the magic mirror.
The queen was cross.
She wanted to be the fairest.

"Who is the fairest?"

The queen sent for a hunter to kill
Snow White.
But he did not want to kill her.
So the hunter left her in the forest.

Snow White was lost in the forest.

Snow White was lost.

Then Snow White saw a cottage.
She went inside.
There were seven little chairs.
There were seven little bowls.

Upstairs there were seven little beds.
Soon Snow White fell asleep.

Snow White saw a cottage.

When Snow White woke up, she saw
seven dwarfs.
"Who are you?" they said.
Snow White told the dwarfs about the
wicked queen.
"You can stay with us," they said.

The next day, the dwarfs went to work.
"Goodbye," said the dwarfs. "You will
be safe here."

She saw seven dwarfs.

But the wicked queen looked in her
magic mirror.
"Who is the fairest?" said the queen.
"Snow White," said the magic mirror.
The queen was cross.
The hunter did not kill Snow White.
"I will kill Snow White myself," said
the wicked queen.

"Who is the fairest?"

The wicked queen put poison in
an apple.
She dressed up as an old woman.
She went to the dwarfs' cottage to
find Snow White.
"Here is an apple," she said.
"Thank you," said Snow White.

"Here is an apple."

"Bite the apple," said the
wicked queen.
Snow White bit the apple.
Then Snow White fell down.
"Snow White is dead!" said
the queen. "Now I am the fairest!"

Snow White fell down.

The dwarfs came home from work.
They saw Snow White.
They tried to wake her up.
But it was no good.
The dwarfs were sad.
"She is dead," they said.
So the dwarfs put Snow White in
a glass coffin.

The dwarfs were sad.

One day, a prince rode by.
He saw Snow White.
The prince kissed Snow White.
And Snow White woke up.
Soon Snow White and
the prince were married.
Everyone was happy.
But the wicked queen was
so cross that she broke her
magic mirror.

Snow White and the prince
were married.

Look back in your book.

Can you read these words?

Snow White

dwarfs

mirror

apple

forest

prince

Can you answer these questions?

Who had a magic mirror?

What did the wicked queen give to Snow White?

How many dwarfs were there?

First Readers

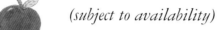

(subject to availability)

Beauty and the Beast
Chicken Licken
Cinderella
The Elves and the Shoemaker
The Emperor's New Clothes
The Enormous Turnip
The Gingerbread Man
Goldilocks and the Three Bears
Hansel and Gretel
Jack and the Beanstalk
Little Red Riding Hood
The Princess and the Pea
Rapunzel
Rumpelstiltskin
Sleeping Beauty
Snow White and the Seven Dwarfs
The Three Billy Goats Gruff
The Three Little Pigs
The Ugly Duckling